Lorna Look-a-lot

Irene Howat

for Georgia

Christian Focus Publications

Mrs Lorna Look-a-lot was always looking at things. Everywhere she went she looked to see what she could see.

Lorna Look-a-lot's dog was called Sniff. He sometimes sniffed out interesting things for her to look at.

Mrs Lorna Look-a-lot took her children to the seaside on holiday. 'There will be lots to look at,' she told them. Liz and Les grinned at each other.

'We packed our magnifying glass,' they said.

'Look!' said Mrs Lorna Look-a-lot, pointing at marks on the smooth sand. 'There's a worm under there.'

Les scraped the sand away. And they all looked at the worm through the magnifying glass.

'Ooo!' said Liz.

'Look!' said Mrs Lorna Look-a-lot, as they ate candyfloss. 'Look at that!'

Liz looked at the candyfloss through the magnifying glass. 'Wow! she said. 'It looks like a huge bowl of pink spaghetti!'

'Look!' said Mrs Lorna Look-a-lot, as they walked along the path. 'Look at the ants!'

Les looked at the ants through the magnifying glass.

'Phew!' he said. 'They're carrying leaves bigger than themselves!'

'Look!' said Mrs Lorna Look-a-lot, pointing to a tree. 'A spider has caught his tea!'

Liz looked at the web through the magnifying glass.

'He's caught a tiny fly,' she said.

'Yuck!' yelped Les.

'Look!' said Mrs Lorna Look-a-lot, very late that night.

Liz and Les looked up and saw thousands of stars.

They walked along the sand in the dark to see them better.

'Look!' yelled the twins. But Mrs Lorna Look-a-lot didn't look where she was going. She tripped over Sniff and landed, splat, on top of a huge sand castle with a flag on top.

'Are you hurt?' Liz and Les asked together. 'No,' smiled Mrs Lorna Look-a-lot, 'but look at this.'

They got down on their knees and looked in a puddle of sea water. It was clear as a mirror and they saw the stars in it.

Suddenly Sniff ran off.

'Hurry!' said Mrs Lorna Look-a-lot.

'He may have found something interesting.'

He had.

They found Sniff beside a hot-dog stand.

So they ate hot-dogs in the starlight before going back to their hotel.

God made all the wonderful things we can see,
and all the tiny things we need to look at through a
magnifying glass.

Dear Father in heaven,

thank you for all the wonderful things you have made. Help me to look at your wonderful little things as well as your wonderful big things. And help me to say thank-you for them all.

Amen.

'God saw all that he had made, and it was very good.' Genesis 1:31

'I lift up my eyes to the hills - where does my help come from? My help comes from the Lord, the Maker of heaven and earth.' Psalm 121:1-2

Collect the Little Lots Series and answer these questions

Lucy Lie-a-lot

Where are the goldfish
called Round and About?

Harry Help-a-lot

What does Cheery Boy
the canary like to do?

Bobby Boast-a-lot

Is Champion the bravest
dog around?

Granny Grump-a-lot

How many mice has
Hunter the cat caught?

Lorna Look-a-lot

What interesting thing
has Sniff the dog found?

William Work-a-lot

How did Stuff the
hamster get his name?

Published by Christian Focus Publications,
Geanies House, Fearn, Tain, Ross-shire, IV20 1TW, Scotland.
www.christianfocus.com © Copyright 2005 Irene Howat Illustrated by Michel de Boer * Printed in the U.K.
The Little Lots series looks at positive and negative characteristics and values.
These titles will help children understand what God wants from our everyday lives. Other titles in this series include:
Lucy Lie-a-lot, Granny Grump-a-lot, William Work-a-lot, Harry Help-a-lot and Bobby Boast-a-lot.